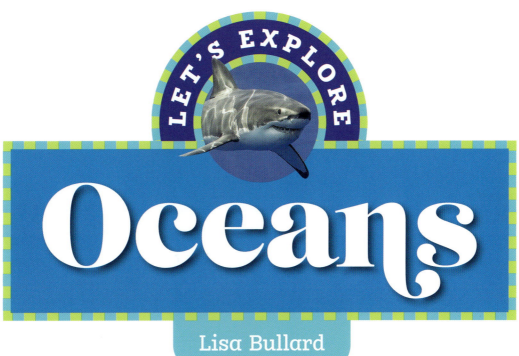

# Oceans

Lisa Bullard

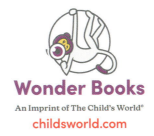

**Wonder Books**
An Imprint of The Child's World®
childsworld.com

**Published by The Child's World®**
800-599-READ • childsworld.com

**Copyright © 2023 by The Child's World®**
All Rights reserved. No part of this book may be reproduced or utilized in any form of by any means without written permission from the publisher.

**Photography Credits**
Photographs ©: H. Tanaka/Shutterstock Images, cover (background), 3 (background); Shutterstock Images, cover (shark), 1, 3 (shark), back cover; Igor Karpenko/Shutterstock Images, 2, 12; Shutterstock Images, 4, 4–5; Ramon Carretero/Shutterstock Images, 6, 11; Rattiya Thongdumhyu/Shutterstock Images, 7; Andrew Sutton/Shutterstock Images, 8; Shutterstock Images, 15; NOAA Office of Ocean Exploration and Research, 16; Robert McGillivray/Shutterstock Images, 19; Dudarev Mikhail/Shutterstock Images, 20, 21; Red Line Editorial, 22

**ISBN Information**
9781503858008 (Reinforced Library Binding)
9781503860339 (Portable Document Format)
9781503861695 (Online Multi-user eBook)
9781503863057 (Electronic Publication)

**LCCN** 2021952486

**Printed in the United States of America**

**Lisa Bullard** is the author of over 100 books for children. She also teaches writing classes for adults and children. Bullard grew up in Minnesota and now lives just north of Minneapolis.

# Contents

**CHAPTER ONE**
**What Is an Ocean Ecosystem?** ....................... 4

**CHAPTER TWO**
**What Lives in or near Oceans?** ................. 6

**CHAPTER THREE**
**Protecting Oceans** ........... 20

Make an Ocean in a Bottle . . . 22
Glossary . . . 23
Find Out More . . . 24
Index . . . 24

## CHAPTER ONE

# What Is an Ocean Ecosystem?

An ocean is a large area of salt water. Earth has five named oceans. They are the Pacific, Atlantic, Indian, Southern, and Arctic Oceans.

Many plants and animals live in the open ocean, which is far away from land. Some of the largest ocean animals live in this huge **ecosystem**.

Plants and animals live at different depths in the ocean. Some remain near the surface. Sunlight reaches those places. Other creatures make their homes many miles deep. But all these living things play a role in keeping the ocean healthy.

Oceans cover about 71 percent of Earth's surface.

# CHAPTER TWO

# What Lives in or near Oceans?

## PHYTOPLANKTON

Phytoplankton (FY-toh-plank-tun) are tiny **algae**. They float in the ocean. They are so small that they can only be seen using a microscope. But they play a huge role as the base of many ocean food webs. Phytoplankton are eaten by small creatures. Those small creatures are eaten by bigger ones. Without phytoplankton, small animals would not have enough food. This would affect the larger animals, too.

Land animals also depend on phytoplankton. These **organisms** produce oxygen. Not all of this oxygen stays in the ocean. Land animals use it to breathe.

Similar to plants, phytoplankton use sunlight to make food.

Blue whales can swim faster than 20 miles per hour (32 kmh) for short bursts.

# BLUE WHALES

Blue whales can grow to be 110 feet (34 m) long. These animals can weigh as much as 330,000 pounds (150,000 kg). This makes them the largest animals on Earth.

Despite their size, blue whales help some of the smallest organisms in the ocean. The whales' waste contains **nutrients**. Phytoplankton use these nutrients to grow.

Although blue whales are huge, most of their food is a tiny, shrimplike animal called krill. A blue whale can eat 40 million krill a day.

DID YOU KNOW?

# GREAT WHITE SHARKS

Great white sharks are one of the biggest ocean **predators**. Few animals eat great white sharks. But the sharks eat many different ocean animals. By doing this, the sharks keep **prey** animal numbers from growing too large. This keeps the food web in balance.

Sharks also help make groups of prey animals stronger. Sharks often go after animals that are sick or weak. Killing these animals keeps diseases from spreading. This means that stronger animals are the ones who survive.

Great white sharks have about seven rows of teeth. They have a total of around 300 teeth.

Jellyfish are about 95 percent water.

# JELLYFISH

Jellyfish are not really fish. They are animals that do not have blood, bones, or a brain. Jellyfish are mostly made of water.

There are at least 200 kinds of jellyfish. They are found in all the world's oceans. Often, they are the predators in a food web. They eat things such as krill and small fish. Sometimes jellyfish become prey to animals like leatherback sea turtles. But sometimes jellyfish are protectors. Young fish sometimes hide among jellyfish **tentacles** to escape from predators.

Jellyfish have stinging cells lining their tentacles. This helps them catch prey.

DID YOU KNOW?

# BLOBFISH

Some animals live their whole lives in very deep parts of the ocean. The blobfish is one of them. It is not easy for scientists to study deep-sea creatures. But they believe that blobfish float just above the ocean floor. They do not hunt their food. They wait for food to pass by. This might include crabs or sea urchins.

# OCEAN ZONES

**Sunlight Zone: Surface to 656 feet (200 m) deep**

**Twilight Zone: 656 to 3,280 feet (200 to 1,000 m) deep**

**Midnight Zone: 3,280 to 13,123 feet (1,000 to 4,000 m) deep**

**The Abyss: 13,123 to 19,685 feet (4,000 to 6,000 m) deep**

**The Trenches: 19,685 to 36,201 feet (6,000 to 11,034 m) deep**

Scientists break the ocean into five zones. Sunlight can only reach the first two zones. The three lower zones are known as the deep ocean.

Sea pigs have pinkish or see-through bodies.

# SEA PIGS

Sea pigs are a type of sea cucumber. Sea cucumbers have long, soft bodies. They live near the bottom of the ocean. People sometimes describe sea pigs as the vacuum cleaners of the ocean. They walk along the deep ocean floor. They dig into the mud for food.

Sea pigs eat dead things that have settled there, such as algae or a dead whale. By eating these things, sea pigs help keep the ocean floor clean.

Sea pigs also help baby king crabs. Young crabs ride along on the bellies or sides of sea pigs. Scientists believe the crabs are using the sea pigs to hide from predators.

# WANDERING ALBATROSSES

The wandering albatross is a very large seabird. Its wingspan can reach 11 feet (3.4 m). Albatrosses sometimes go years without ever touching land. They spend much of their time flying over the ocean waves. But they still depend on the ocean for food. They land on the water's surface to catch their prey. This might include squid or fish.

Albatrosses also poop into the ocean. Their poop puts nutrients back into the water. This helps feed ocean ecosystems.

**DID YOU KNOW?**

The wandering albatross can smell its prey from as far as 12 miles (19.3 km) away.

Wandering albatrosses can be found near Antarctica.

# Protecting Oceans

Ocean animals are not the only ones that depend on the ocean. The ocean also affects Earth's **climate**. The sun heats ocean waters. This warm water is carried around the world as these waters move. Heated water also rises into the air. It turns into rain.

People must work to keep the ocean healthy. Governments make laws to protect oceans. Groups raise money to help ocean animals. Individuals can also do their part. Recycling or reusing items prevents waste that could wind up in the ocean. A balanced ocean ecosystem is important. It keeps many different organisms healthy.

Less than 20 percent of the ocean has been explored.

# Make an Ocean in a Bottle

The ocean is known for its waves. You can create your own ocean waves in a bottle.

**Materials**
- Bottle with a lid
- Water
- Blue food coloring
- Baby oil or cooking oil
- Small toy fish or boats (optional)

## Directions

1. Fill the bottle ¼ of the way with water.
2. Add one or two drops of food coloring to turn the water blue like an ocean.
3. Put any toy fish or boats into the bottle.
4. Carefully fill the rest of the bottle with oil. Try not to leave any space at the top. Ask an adult if you need help.
5. Put the lid on the bottle. Screw it tightly so the bottle will not leak.
6. Carefully turn the bottle on its side. Rock the bottle back and forth. The water will look like waves in the ocean.

# Glossary

**algae** (AL-jee) Algae are plantlike organisms that grow in water and make food using sunlight. Phytoplankton are a type of algae.

**climate** (KLY-muht) The climate is the weather over a long period of time in a particular area. The ocean affects Earth's climate.

**ecosystem** (EE-koh-siss-tuhm) An ecosystem is all of the living and nonliving things in an area. Animals affect their ecosystem.

**nutrients** (NOO-tree-uhnts) Nutrients are substances that help living things grow. Most vegetables are full of nutrients.

**organisms** (OR-guh-nih-zuhms) Organisms are life-forms, including all plants and animals. Phytoplankton are tiny organisms.

**predators** (PREH-duh-turz) Predators are animals that hunt and eat other animals. Great white sharks are some of the ocean's largest predators.

**prey** (PRAY) Prey are animals that other animals hunt and eat. Jellyfish are prey for leatherback sea turtles.

**tentacles** (TEN-tuh-culls) Tentacles are flexible arms some creatures have. Jellyfish have tentacles.

# Find Out More

### In the Library

Baker, Miranda. *Ultimate Earth: Oceans and Seas*. Wilton, CT: 360 Degrees, 2021.

London, Martha. *Looking Into the Ocean*. Mankato, MN: The Child's World, 2020.

Wilsdon, Christina. *Ultimate Oceanpedia: The Most Complete Ocean Reference Ever*. Washington, DC: National Geographic Children's Books, 2016.

### On the Web

Visit our website for links about oceans:
**childsworld.com/links**

*Note to Parents, Teachers, and Librarians: We routinely verify our Web links to make sure they are safe and active sites. So encourage your readers to check them out!*

# Index

algae, 6, 17

climate, 20

ecosystem, 4, 18, 20

great white sharks, 10

jellyfish, 13

nutrients, 9, 18

ocean zones, 15

organisms, 6, 9, 20

phytoplankton, 6, 9

predators, 10, 13, 17

prey, 10, 13, 18, 19

tentacles, 13